THE HAUNTING OF PIP PAR[KER]

It's Christmas Eve and Pip can't s[leep]. But not because she's excited; she's scared!

Anne Fine has been elected [...] e on the prestigious position of Children's Laureate in 2001. A highly acclaimed author, she has won the Smarties Book Prize, the Guardian Children's Fiction Award and has twice won the Carnegie Medal and the Whitbread Children's Book Award. She was also voted Children's Author of the Year in 1990 and 1993. Her book *Goggle-eyes* was dramatized as a BBC TV serial and *Madame Doubtfire* was turned into the hugely successful Hollywood film, *Mrs Doubtfire*. She has two daughters and lives in County Durham.

You can find out more about Anne Fine and her books by visiting her website, at www.annefine.co.uk

Books by the same author

Care of Henry

ANNE FINE

THE HAUNTING OF

PIP PARKER

Illustrations by
Emma Chichester Clark

WALKER BOOKS
AND SUBSIDIARIES

LONDON · BOSTON · SYDNEY · AUCKLAND

Story first published 1991 in the
Telegraph Magazine as "All I Want for Christmas"

This edition published 2001 by
Walker Books Ltd, 87 Vauxhall Walk
London SE11 5HJ

2 4 6 8 10 9 7 5 3

This book has been typeset in Garamond

Printed and bound in Great Britain by J.H. Haynes & Co. Ltd

British Library Cataloguing in Publication Data:
a catalogue record for this book is
available from the British Library

ISBN 0-7445-8294-6

www.walkerbooks.co.uk

For David Irwin
A.F.

Maybe you're braver than I am.
Maybe it wouldn't spoil your
Christmas Eve to have to lie
awake feeling haunted,
instead of drifting off
to sleep knowing
you'd wake
to find your
stocking
full of
presents.

Maybe you wouldn't mind the night before Christmas being turned into a sort of two-months-late Hallowe'en.

I minded. I minded a lot.

Over there on my desk lay the gifts I'd made…

or saved to buy…

and wrapped up for other people.

11

Down there at the end
of my bed, across
my feet, lay my big
red (still empty)
Christmas
stocking.

Above my head hung the glittery
Advent calendar I'd made at school,
with only one door left to open.

And there, on the far wall,
was what was keeping me
awake – the horrible tiny
golden skull shape that
had been shining at
me off the wall for
a whole week.

Maybe you have stronger nerves than I do. But I couldn't sleep. And I'm not a baby. I managed well enough when I slept over at Great Aunt Belle's, and the branches of her ash tree waved in front of the street light and threw the creepiest shadows you've ever seen over the bedroom wall.

I was fine at Alex's house too, even if it did take me a bit of time to work out that those weird snaky things that kept flitting across the ceiling were just car headlights turning into Mappin Road.

But here in my own home I was a
total wreck. I shut my eyes to go to
sleep, and had to keep opening
them again, to see if the
skull was still

watching me. Not that it had eyes, exactly. It was just a shape on the wall, a gleaming shape, about the size of my thumb. But it worried me. I couldn't take my eyes off it. And so I couldn't get to sleep, and all week I'd been going around like a zombie, too tired even to think.

And they all kept asking me things.

Pips, what was the name of that rather nasty plastic thing you saw in the shop window and liked so much?

It's Granny on the phone. She wants to know if Pip likes poetry. Do you like poetry, Pip?

Simply as a matter of interest, Pip, did you ever find your bike chain?

I'd try to concentrate. After all, I know as well as you do that it's important to keep your wits about you when people are asking you this sort of question in the last few days before Christmas. Too many wrong answers, and you can fetch up with a pile of junk.

But I was too sleepy to think. And yawning so hard, I couldn't answer anyway.

"Pip! There's only a couple of days left. Please give us a few ideas. What sort of things would you like?"

"Books?"

"Clothes?"

"Pens?"

"Cassettes?"

"Computer stuff?"

Already I was deep in another yawn.

"Pip!"

I made a real effort. But all I wanted for Christmas was to stop being haunted. And that's what I told them.

"All I want for Christmas is for someone to get rid of that horrible thing on my bedroom wall."

"There's nothing on your wall."

"Oh yes, there is!"

"No, there isn't. It's all your imagination. Three times the whole lot of us have trooped upstairs to look for it for you. And every single time there was nothing there."

It came back as soon as you'd gone.

I can't help it. When I get tired, I get scratchy-tempered. That's just the way I am. I need my sleep. And so, all through last week, when they kept asking me, "Have you decided what you want for Christmas yet?", I kept saying over and over (though I knew how it was annoying them):

You could hear their voices going all frosty. "Right, then. I suppose it will just have to be a surprise."

No one believed me. Nobody offered to come up and have another look. And I could see their point.

After all, it was true that they'd been up three times already. Three evenings in a row, when I came down in my pyjamas to complain, they'd all laid their drinks down with a sigh and trooped up the stairs, one after another, moaning.

I'll tell you Pip's problem.
Too much television.

It was there, though. Oh, yes. It was there gleaming at me, as it had been all week. I knew I could go down one last time, but they'd probably get ratty, and might even start teasing me again about the snack Granny had insisted on leaving out "for Santa".

No, I was better off up in my bedroom, lying awake staring at the wall and wondering just how the horrible gleaming little skull shape knew exactly when to fold up and disappear.

The last person in the family to come up and have a look was my

mother. I heard her hurrying up the stairs and along the landing towards my bedroom, not even stopping to admire the new lamp she'd bought so that Granny could get from the spare room to the bathroom without tripping over the frayed patches in the carpet.

Then she burst through my door.

"Where is it, then?"

And, of course, it had vanished.

"It was here just a moment ago. I was watching it. Honestly."

"Oh, Pip!"

"Just stay a few minutes. Keep absolutely quiet, and see if you can fool it into coming back."

Sighing, she leaned back against the door, and waited.

The seconds passed.

Bored and impatient, she started to drum her fingers behind her on the panels of the door.

"Sssh!" I warned.

She was quiet.

A few more seconds passed. Then.
"Pip! I can't stay here all night. Either
it's here, or it isn't. And it isn't."

"But it was here. Only a minute
ago."

She swung the door open again,
and went out.

"I'll shut this behind me," she

said. "So the noise from downstairs doesn't keep you awake."

"I'll be awake anyway," I told her. But she'd already gone.

And she was no more than a few
steps along the landing before I
turned back, and there it was again!
On the wall...
Gleaming at me...

And that's when I did exactly
what you would do. I gave up.
I gave up trying to have a normal
Christmas Eve. I gave up trying
to sleep.

I simply lay in bed and waited.

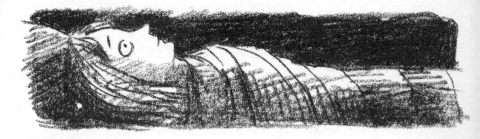

And waited.

And waited.

And waited and waited and waited.

And that's
how I came to
stay awake longer
than anyone else my
age, ever, on Christmas Eve.
That's how, when I heard the
rustling outside, and the rattle of
my doorknob, I quickly closed my
eyes and pretended as hard as I
could that I was fast asleep.

I'm not daft. And I wanted my
stocking filled.

I have to tell you, if you didn't
know, that Santa's not quite as
portly as he looks in most of the
pictures you see about. It wasn't
easy to tell in the dark, but if you

want my opinion he's no fatter
than my father. He's no taller
either. And he uses much the same
language when he stubs his toe
against the bedstead.

However, unlike my father, he brought me all I want for Christmas. And this is how.

First, he stepped down to the bottom of my bed. I could hear the rustle of presents being stuffed in my stocking. I thought I'd be safer if I turned my face away. You never know.

I'm sure I'm as good as you are at pretending I'm fast asleep, but you know as well as I do that, once you think someone might be watching you, even in the dark, you get this urge to grin.

So I made a sort of fast-asleep, lip-smacking sound and rolled over restlessly to face the other way.

It was safe to open my eyes now. And there, on the wall, was the gleaming little skull shape.

Behind me, the heavy footsteps went back towards the door.

The skull shape disappeared.

Did I move my foot? I'm sure
I didn't move my foot, but it is
true that, just at that moment, my
Christmas stocking slipped off the
bed on to the floor.

The footsteps came back down
to the bottom of my bed again.

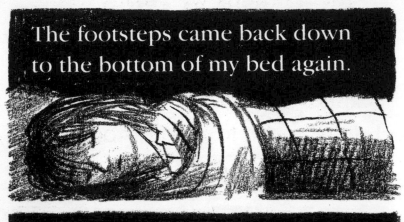

The skull shape reappeared.
I felt a fumbling round my feet.

Then my stocking was laid
down on top of them.

The footsteps went back to the door. The shape on the wall vanished.

I moved my foot – only a tiny bit. I didn't mean to tip the stocking on to the floor again.

I won't tell you what Santa muttered. You wouldn't want to know, and, if you did, your family wouldn't want you to repeat it.

The footsteps came back down to the end of the bed.

The skull shape reappeared. The stocking landed on the bed again. (Quite hard.)

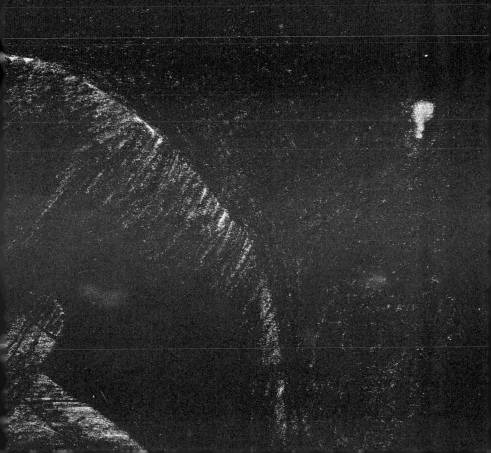

The footsteps went back to the
door. The skull shape vanished.

And suddenly, instantly, in a
flash, I had all I wanted for
Christmas! And I don't mean
a stocking full of presents.

No! I didn't care if what was
crushing my feet was wonderful
presents I'd longed for all my life,
or just some old heap of bike
chains and poetry books and winter
clothes. (To be perfectly honest
with you, even now I haven't
bothered to pull them out of the
stocking and unwrap them.)

No. All I did was slip out of bed, pad over to the door in my bare feet, and stuff that stupid skull-shaped keyhole so full of torn up scraps of wrapping paper that no light would ever again be able to shine through from the other side and make gleaming shapes on my wall.

Maybe you're brighter than I am. Maybe you would have cottoned on the very first evening, and known straight away that the new lamp on the landing was to blame.

Maybe you would have realized at once that the reason nobody else could ever see the skull shape on the wall was because they were leaning against the door and blocking the light through the keyhole. Maybe.

Well, you may be brighter than I am, but you couldn't be more tired. I'm going off to sleep now – my first good sleep for a week. Oh, I know the whole lot of them will be at me again in the morning.

It won't do them any good. I won't even be awake to hear. They can go ahead and open their presents without me. I have all I want for Christmas already – a nice blank wall. And that means a good, long, deep and dreamless sleep. I'm starting it right now.

And I shan't give my best present up that easily.

Neither would you.

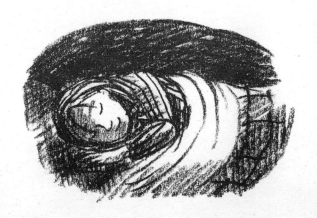

More SPRINTERS for you to enjoy!

- *Little Stupendo Flies High* Jon Blake   0-7445-5970-7

- *Captain Abdul's Pirate School* Colin McNaughton 0-7445-5242-7

- *The Ghost in Annie's Room* Philippa Pearce   0-7445-5993-6

- *Molly and the Beanstalk* Pippa Goodhart   0-7445-5981-2

- *Taking the Cat's Way Home* Jan Mark   0-7445-8268-7

- *The Finger-eater* Dick King-Smith   0-7445-8269-5

- *Care of Henry* Anne Fine   0-7445-8270-9

- *The Impossible Parents Go Green* Brian Patten   0-7445-7881-7

- *Flora's Fantastic Revenge* Nick Warburton   0-7445-7898-1

- *Jolly Roger* Colin McNaughton   0-7445-8293-8

- *The Haunting of Pip Parker* Anne Fine   0-7445-8294-6

- *Tarquin the Wonder Horse* June Crebbin   0-7445-7882-5

All at £3.99